The next moment,
Ted and Dolly
found themselves
in a hot, steamy
jungle.
All around they saw
strange animals
and heard
frightening sounds...

All of a sudden,
they were in a
huge library.
It was very quiet
except for
some grown-ups
saying "shhh...!"

Whoosh! Ted and Dolly were at the North Pole. They looked around and saw one of Ted's cousins.

Suddenly,
Ted and Dolly found
that they were
the main course
at a GIANT'S
tea party...!

Ted and Dolly
had never
seen so much
ice cream...

Their new friends enjoyed helping Ted and Dolly to eat the ice cream...!

And in a moment
they were
tucked up safely
in Lucy's bed...